X

TANA HOBAN

Look Up, Look Down

GREENWILLOW BOOKS NEW YORK

LIBRARY OF CONGRESS CATALOGING-IN-PUBLICATION DATA
HOBAN, TANA.
LOOK UP, LOOK DOWN / BY TANA HOBAN.
P.   CM.
SUMMARY: PHOTOGRAPHS PRESENT OBJECTS AND SCENES FROM DIFFERENT
PERSPECTIVES, SOME VIEWED FROM BELOW AND SOME FROM ABOVE.
ISBN 0-688-10577-7 (TRADE).   ISBN 0-688-10578-5 (LIB.)
[1. VISUAL PERCEPTION.]   I. TITLE.   PZ7.H638LOP   1992
[E]—DC20 91-12613 CIP AC

THIS BOOK IS DEDICATED TO

LOVE AND PEACE . . . ALL AROUND THE WORLD

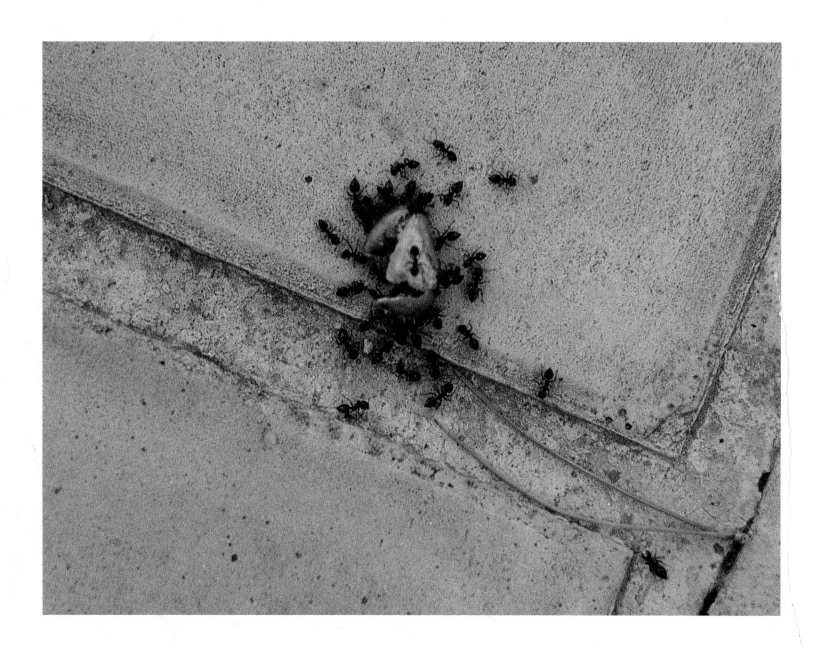

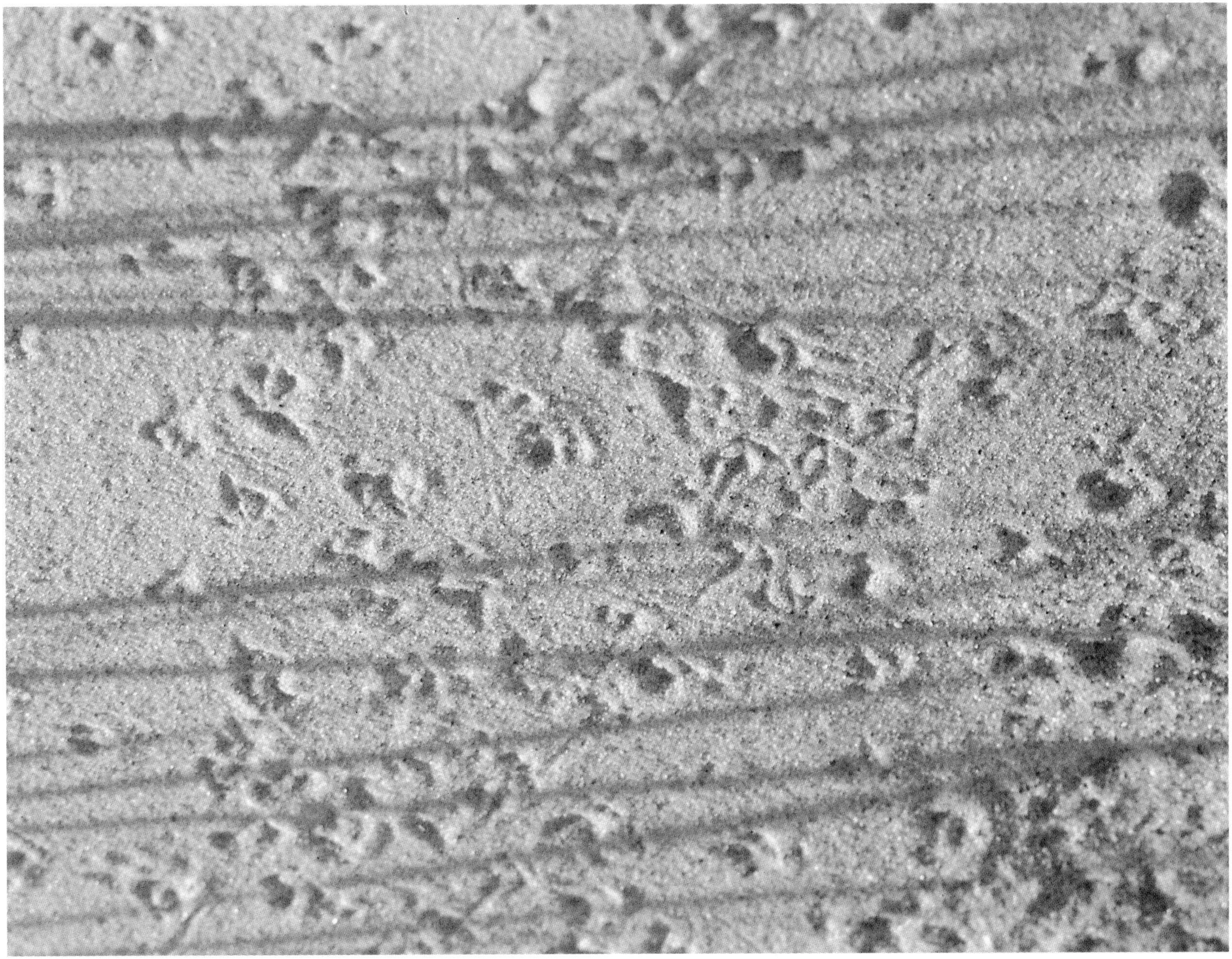

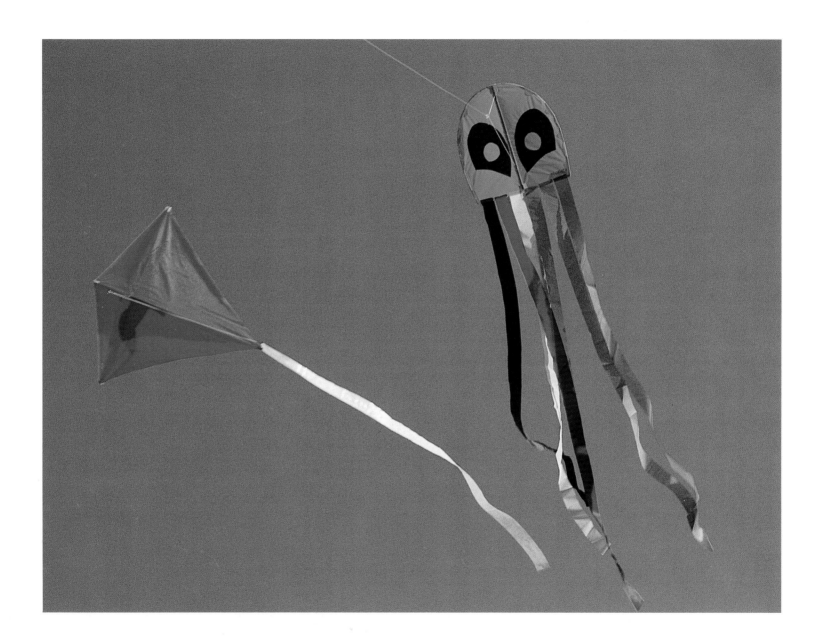

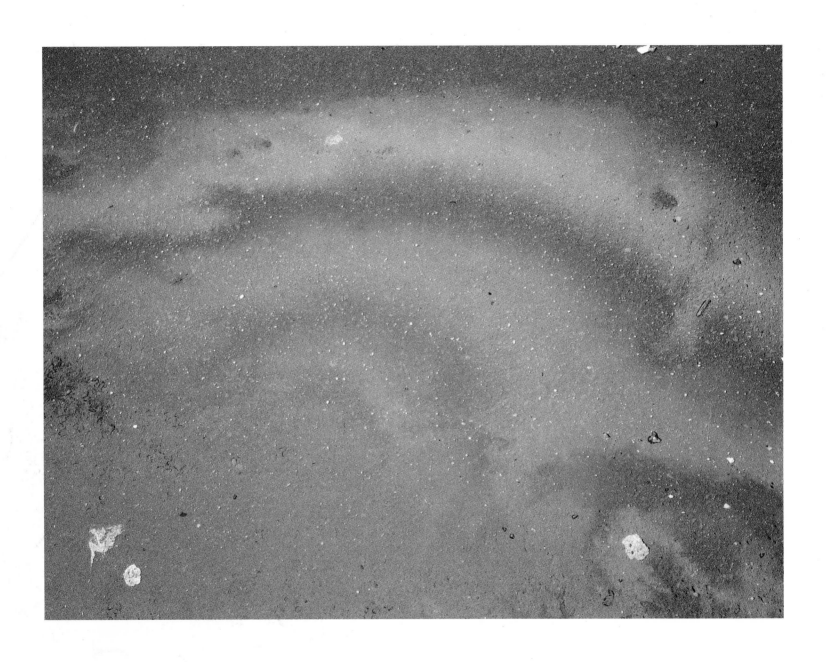